THE THREAD THAT REMAINS

ANISH GHATAK

This book is dedicated to my Ammi. She was the light of my life and someone who originally identified my writing prowess. My facination for fiction and fantasy came because of her. She was academically inclined, extremely lovable and fierce when the situation demanded it. I miss her laughter with every page that I write. May she rest in peace whilst knowing that her dadu bhai has not paused his pen.

I love you Ammi. This one is for you :-)

Contents

Contents

Foreword

To the ones who've carried someone too long in their bones. To the ones who stayed when leaving would've been easier. To the ones who've forgotten themselves to keep someone else whole.

You may find pieces of yourself in this story. Some of them will hurt. Some may heal. None will come back unchanged.

Because love does not vanish. It echoes.

And in places the world forgets, it waits.

Preface

I didn't set out to write a book about grief.

I thought this was going to be a story about shadows and forests and things that watch us when we think we're alone. But the more I wrote, the more I understood something quieter was asking to be seen, the way memory bends us, the way love can become a burden we're both terrified to carry and too afraid to let go of.

This isn't a story about heroes. Elaine isn't here to save the world. She's trying to remember who she is while holding onto someone who no longer does. That weight of being remembered wrong, of being left behind while still present, is the real ghost haunting these pages.

If this book reaches you at a time when you're carrying someone in silence, or holding onto something that keeps slipping away, I hope you find in it the kind of stillness that lets you breathe again.

Thank you for stepping into the fog.

Acknowledgements

To the ones who held space for this story, thank you. To the long nights, the quiet mornings, and the faces I wrote for even when they didn't know. To memory, for refusing to fade.

To my parents, for supporting me throughout this endeavour. Your belief in me carried this through the fog.

And to every reader who sees themselves somewhere between these pages. You are not alone.

Prologue

Before the first door opened, there was only memory.

Not the clean kind. Not the ones wrapped in sunlight and laughter. These were the jagged, raw ones, the ones that kept people awake and made them whisper names to empty rooms.

Somewhere, across the boundary of time and forgetting, someone wanted to let go of what hurt. But the world has rules. And memory, once traded, never disappears.

It waits.

In stone. In fog. In the shape of someone you once loved.

This is a story of such a memory. A girl who wouldn't stop remembering. A boy who chose to forget. And the thing that waited between them.

This is the thread that remains.

Act 1

1

The Watcher on the Hill

The wind cut through the hills of Wayward Hollow, sharp and bitter. The crescent moon hung low, its pale light stretching across the desolate ridge. Somewhere, a wolf howled. The sound faded into stillness.

Below, among the ancient oaks, the village of Grimwater slept behind shuttered windows and bolted doors. Smoke curled from chimneys. No one walked the streets. The night, here, was something to fear.

Only one figure moved.

Elaine Thornwood stood atop Widow's Ridge, her cloak snapping in the wind. One hand gripped a lantern, its flicker barely holding against the dark. In the other, a hunting knife. Not for wolves. For worse.

The Watcher was out tonight.

"Elaine, you should be home," came a voice behind her. Deep. Familiar. Worried.

She turned. Corwin. Her brother. Dark hair tousled. Storm-gray eyes matching her own.

"Couldn't sleep," she said, watching the valley. The knife in her hand caught the moonlight. "Neither could you."

He stepped closer. "That doesn't mean you should be up here alone."

"They say the Watcher walks the hills when the moon is high," she said. "Preys on the foolish. And the brave."

She glanced at him, a flicker of a smile. "Which are we?"

"Reckless," he muttered. But he didn't leave.

Together, they scanned the village below. Quiet. Still. Then..

A creak. Wood shifting.

Elaine stiffened. "Did you hear that?"

Corwin nodded. His hand moved to their father's blade, strapped at his side. A relic from before Grimwater was a village. From when steel still mattered.

A ripple in the dark. Shadow against shadow.

It stepped from the trees.

Tall. Too tall. Thin as bone. Its face smooth and pale, empty but for two hollow eyes glowing faintly.

The Watcher.

"Gods," Corwin whispered.

Elaine gripped his arm. "We have to warn them."

"Warn them of what? A ghost? They won't listen. They'll call us mad."

She didn't flinch. "Then we face it. We know what it does."

He hesitated. Then nodded. "No rushing in."

"Smart," she said. Her heart was hammering, but her mind stayed clear.

The Watcher paused at the forest's edge. Tilted its head. Listening.

Then it moved.

Corwin drew his sword. Elaine raised the lantern higher.

They moved together, down the ridge.

The forest deepened. Cold thickened. The Watcher walked like silence itself. It turned. Saw them.

Its eyes locked onto Elaine.

A glow. A whisper in her mind.

Come closer.

She jerked her head, breath catching. "Don't look at it," she warned.

But Corwin stepped forward, sword raised. "Stay back! You won't take her!"

The Watcher tilted its head.

Then it lunged.

Elaine screamed. Ran to Corwin.

The shadows swallowed them whole.

And in the dark, a single thought burned:

This is only the beginning

2

The Whispering Dark

Elaine gasped awake. Taste of blood in her mouth. Cold dirt beneath her. Her cloak clung, soaked through. Her knife was gone. Her lantern is gone.

"Corwin?" she called. No answer. Her voice scraped the dark.

All around her, the forest twisted. Thick fog smothered sight. Branches curled overhead like skeletal hands.

She forced herself up. Legs shaking. Hands searching.

"Corwin!"

Silence.

The Watcher. She remembered its hollow eyes. The way it moved. Then nothing.

The quiet gnawed at her.

She walked. Fog heavy. Roots snaking beneath her feet.

Then the sound came.

Whispers.

At first, distant. Then rising. Not one voice—many. A language she didn't know but felt in her bones.

She pressed forward. "You won't scare me," she whispered.

The whispering grew.

You cannot run. You cannot hide. You will see.

"Stop it!" she shouted. The forest fell silent.

Then the sound of groaning. Something dragging.

Her breath caught. She spun. No weapon. Nowhere to hide.

"Corwin? Please, tell me it's you."

Out of the mist, a figure.

Corwin.

Limping. Pale. Eyes glazed. Blood on his side.

Behind him, the Watcher.

Elaine froze. The creature lingered just beyond reach. Watching.

"Run!" she shouted.

Corwin stumbled forward. Silent. Haunted. The Watcher raised one spindly arm.

You will see. You will understand.

Elaine ran to Corwin, grabbed him, and pulled. His skin—ice. His movement—barely there.

The Watcher didn't follow. It just watched it.

She didn't stop until the air eased and the whispers dulled.

Corwin collapsed.

Wounded. Breathing shallow.

"Stay with me," she said, pressing the wound. "I'll fix this."

He rasped, "It spoke to me. Said my name."

Her blood ran cold.

Then the voice returned.

"You will not escape. You belong to us."

Fog thickened. Shadows moved.

And the hunt began.

3

The Hunt Begins

Elaine tightened her grip on Corwin's arm. His breath was shallow. His skin is cold. The Watcher's words rang in her mind like iron struck on stone.

She pressed harder on the wound. Blood leaked between her fingers.

"Stay with me," she whispered. "I've got you."

Corwin winced. "It's inside me," he rasped. "Crawling... whispering."

She swallowed hard. The fog thickened. The forest leaned in.

Footsteps.

Slow. Deliberate.

The Watcher was coming.

Elaine scanned the ground. A shard of stone. Jagged. Sharp enough.

She grabbed it.

The footsteps stopped. Just beyond the fog.

Elaine bent close. "Corwin. Move. Please."

His eyes fluttered open. Glazed. He muttered, "Leave me."

"No," she said. "Not this time."

A silhouette formed. The Watcher. Watching.

Elaine stood.

Stone in hand. "Stay away!" she shouted.

The creature tilted its head.

Why fight? He is ours. You will follow.

Elaine stepped forward.

The Watcher lunged.

She slashed. The stone scraped its arm. It hissed.

Not invincible.

Then it struck back. She flew. Hit the ground hard. Wind knocked out.

It towered over her. Eyes burning.

A horn blared.

The Watcher paused. Turned.

Torches.

Figures moved through the trees. Cloaked. Armed.

The Watcher hissed. Melted into shadow.

Elaine barely breathed until hands reached her.

A man knelt. Cloaked. Stern. "You're lucky to be alive," he said. He looked to Corwin. "Both of you."

Elaine tried to speak. Her voice failed.

The man nodded to others. They lifted Corwin.

"Who are you?" she whispered.

"Hunters," the man said. "Tracking the thing that found you."

Elaine faded. Darkness pulled her under.

His voice followed.

"Rest. You're safe. For now."

4

The Unseen Price

Elaine woke to the firelight. Her body ached like she'd been dragged through stone. The air smelled of smoke, herbs, and blood.

She sat up too fast. Pain sliced through her ribs.

"Corwin?"

"He's alive," said a voice from the shadows.

The man from the forest. Cloaked. Watchful. Scarred.

Elaine's eyes darted to a nearby cot.

Corwin lay still. Pale. Breathing, but shallow. Bandages dark with blood.

She moved to stand.

The man stepped in her way. "He's not safe. Not yet."

"What do you mean?"

"You felt it," the man said. "The mark."

Elaine's heart thudded. "What mark?"

"The Watcher touched him. Left something behind."

Elaine shook her head. "No. We got away."

"Physically? Yes." The man's voice was cold. "But the thing that touched him didn't leave empty-handed. It planted itself. A thread. And that thread leads back to him."

She stared at Corwin. He twitched in his sleep. His lips moved. Whispering something only he could hear.

"How do we stop it?"

"We cut the thread." The man turned to a table and picked up a vial filled with black liquid. It shimmered like oil.

Elaine's voice dropped. "What happens if we do?"

"He lives."

Her breath caught. "And?"

The man didn't flinch. "He forgets. Everything. Including you."

Elaine froze.

"He'll survive," the man said. "But your bond, the one the Watcher used to find him, will be gone. It's the only way."

She turned to Corwin. Remembered the river. The sword lessons. The stories whispered late into the night. Every thread that made them who they were.

Her voice cracked. "Is there another way?"

"If there is, I don't know."

Elaine knelt. Took Corwin's hand. It was cold. She held it anyway.

"I'm here," she whispered. "I'm still here."

The man stepped closer. "If you love him, choose now."

Elaine looked up, eyes wet. "Do it."

The man uncorked the vial.

"Hold him," he said.

Elaine gripped Corwin's hand tighter.

The whispers returned. Louder than ever.

You belong to us.

The liquid poured. Smoke rose.

Everything shattered.

5

Threads in the Dark

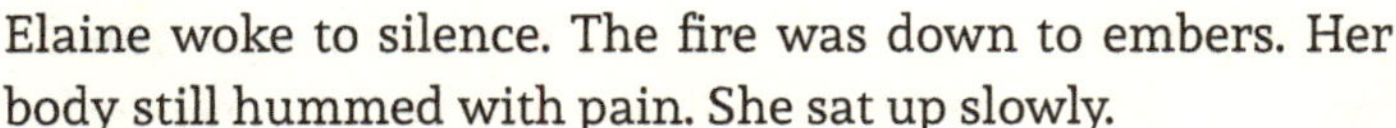

Elaine woke to silence. The fire was down to embers. Her body still hummed with pain. She sat up slowly.

Corwin's cot was empty.

Panic seized her. She pushed to her feet and staggered forward.

"You won't find him here," said the man from behind.

Elaine spun. "You said he'd be safe."

"He is," the man said. "He's outside. Alive."

She didn't relax. "The ritual worked?"

"It did. The connection is broken."

"Then why isn't he here?"

The hunter didn't answer immediately. Instead, he moved to the fire, prodded the embers with a stick, and stared into the glow.

Elaine waited.

Finally, he said, "Not the bond. Not what you were to him."

Elaine sat down. Hard.

She knew the price. But hearing it still felt like a blade.

She looked toward the door. "He remembers nothing?"

"Not the bond. Not what you were to him."

Her heart pulled tight. She remembered the river. His voice. His arms around her. A lifetime dissolved by a single choice.

The man stepped closer. "You denied the Watcher its hold. But it isn't done."

Elaine's eyes narrowed. "Will it come back?"

"It always does. But now, it will come for him as a stranger."

"How do I protect someone who doesn't know me?"

"You already did," the man said. "Now you do it again."

Elaine stayed near the fire for a while. The hunter had gone quiet. Outside, she could hear the morning birds begin to stir. Everything felt too normal for what had just happened.

She stood, walked to Corwin's empty cot, and ran her hand along the sheet where his head had rested. It was still warm.

She closed her eyes. Let herself feel it, just for a moment. Not grief. No regret. Something quieter. A hollow acceptance.

Then she stepped outside. The air was crisp. The sky is pale with dawn.

Corwin stood at the treeline, still and quiet.

She walked to him, slow.

He turned.

His storm-gray eyes met hers. Familiar, but distant.

"I don't know who you are," he said softly. "But you feel familiar."

Elaine nodded. "I'm someone who won't leave."

He hesitated. Then said, "Thank you. For... whatever you did."

Elaine didn't cry. She only stood beside him.

The Watcher was out there.

But he was still here.
And that would have to be enough.

6

Ashes Between Us

They walked back in silence. Corwin watched the path with caution, like someone learning the world again. Elaine stayed beside him, heart heavy, words caught in her throat.

Inside, the hunter had cleared the table. He didn't look up.

Corwin's eyes flicked to him. "You're the one who saved me."

The hunter gave a nod. "You were slipping. She wouldn't let go."

Corwin looked at Elaine, puzzled. "I'm sorry. I should remember, shouldn't I?"

Elaine forced a smile. "You remember enough."

But inside, it hurt. Not just forgetting. The way he spoke. Like she was a kind stranger.

Later, as Corwin rested, Elaine sat outside on a fallen log. Her fingers dug into the bark. The trees didn't speak. The wind didn't answer. But inside her, something cracked.

She didn't sob. Didn't break. But her face was still, hollow.

The hunter joined her. He handed her a flask. "Drink. You look like someone who forgot how."

Elaine took it. "Did you lose someone too?"

The hunter didn't answer right away. Then: "My wife. My son. Years ago."

She looked at him.

"They weren't taken by the Watcher," he said. "But the grief? It makes you see shadows even where there are none."

Elaine passed the flask back. "How do you keep going?"

"You don't," he said. "You just walk until it feels like motion again."

They sat in silence.

"I keep thinking," she said quietly, "if I'd been faster. If I'd acted sooner."

He shook his head. "Don't start chasing ghosts. It's the one thing they want."

From inside, Corwin stirred. A distant sound. The hunter stood.

"He'll need to relearn more than memory. Trust. Instinct. You. Be patient."

Elaine nodded. Her fingers curled into her cloak.

When she walked back in, Corwin was awake. Sitting at the edge of the cot. Looking at his hands.

"I don't feel broken," he said. "But I keep thinking I should."

Elaine sat beside him. "Some things don't leave scars. Not the kind you can see."

He looked at her again. "Were we close?"

She smiled, but her eyes shimmered. "You were everything."

He held her gaze. Said nothing.

Outside, the forest was quiet.

But something happened.

Far off, behind roots and fog, the Watcher waited.

It had lost one thread.
But it remembered the shape of her grief.
And it was learning how to use it.

17

7
The Shape of Her Shadow

The mornings were quieter now. Not peaceful. Just quiet in that way where you knew something was watching.

Corwin had started drawing. Not with purpose. Just... shapes. Circles with slashes. Houses with no windows. A tree split down the middle.

Elaine watched from the doorway, arms folded, jaw tight. She didn't ask. She didn't want to know if his hands remembered things his mind had lost.

Later, she found him staring into the water barrel.

"It doesn't feel like my face," he said. "But it doesn't feel like someone else's either."

Elaine wanted to tell him it was the same face that used to grin after stealing her last bite of bread. The one that scrunched when he laughed so hard he cried. She said nothing.

At night, he dreamt loud. Not words. Just breath and broken sounds. Like something was scraping at the edges of him, trying to climb back in.

She couldn't sleep. Not properly. The fire was too soft. The dark is too thick.

The hunter had started sleeping by the door.

"Do you trust him?" Corwin asked one evening.

Elaine nodded. "More than most."

"He seems... tired."

"He's been tired for a long time."

Corwin turned away, but not before she saw it—the flicker of guilt. Like a shadow he didn't know he owned.

That night, she found the hunter outside, sharpening his blade.

"Do you ever stop?" she asked.

He paused. "Stopped once. Didn't like what came after."

Elaine sat beside him. "You said you lost your family."

He nodded.

"You never talk about them."

He looked at the stars. "What's there to say? My son liked making up songs. My wife hated soup. They're gone. I'm not. That's the story."

Elaine swallowed hard. "Sometimes I think I should've let Corwin go. Let the memory fade instead of fighting for what's no longer real."

The hunter didn't look at her. "Then why didn't you?"

She blinked. "Because it felt like losing twice."

A silence fell. But this one wasn't heavy. Just real.

Inside, Corwin spoke in his sleep. Elaine moved closer to the doorway. Listened.

"You left me."

His voice, but not.

Elaine froze. The hunter stood too, slowly, hand on the hilt.

They waited.

Nothing more came.

Just the crackle of fire. The breathing of someone caught between two lives.

Far beyond, in a place no map dared name, something smiled.

It had touched the edge of her sorrow.

And it was coming back.

Act 2

8

The Thing with No Shape

It began with the birds.

Three crows fell from the sky. One after the other. No wounds. No blood. Just empty. As if something had taken the inside and left the skin.

Elaine buried them behind the cabin. Corwin watched in silence.

"You think it's back," he said.

Elaine didn't answer. She didn't need to.

That night, Corwin wandered. Not far. But far enough that when she woke and didn't see him, her breath caught.

She found him near the river, staring into the water. It didn't ripple.

"I dream of fire," he said. "And a house with no doors."

Elaine's throat tightened. "That's not your dream."

Corwin turned. "Then why does it feel familiar?"

The next day, they found the hunter pacing. Not sharpening his blade. Not watching the forest. Searching.

"What is it?" Elaine asked.

He didn't look at her. "I keep a journal. It's missing."

"Maybe you misplaced it."

"I don't misplace things," he said. "Not that."

Corwin leaned against the doorway, arms crossed. "What was in it?"

The hunter hesitated. Then, "Names. Places I've marked. Dreams I've had more than once."

"Dreams?" Elaine asked.

"The Watcher doesn't just feed on fear," he said. "It burrows. Leaves an echo. I write them down so I know what's mine."

Elaine felt it then. That sliver of unease curling beneath her ribs.

Later, she found Corwin asleep by the fire. A sketch beside him.

It was a door. Tall. Crooked. No handle. Beneath it, a shadow.

But it wasn't his shadow.

She reached to take it. His hand caught hers.

"I didn't draw that," he whispered.

Her breath caught. "Then who did?"

He looked at her with eyes that didn't blink.

"I think it was watching through me."

That night, the fire wouldn't catch. The wind whistled through cracks that hadn't been there yesterday. And far off in the trees, something hummed. Not a sound. A feeling.

The hunter didn't sleep. Neither did Elaine.

And Corwin kept whispering in a voice that wasn't his.

"I remember the river."

But he had never said that before.

9

In the Walls of Silence

The next morning brought no sun.

A dim gray hung over the trees like a held breath. Elaine stepped outside and the world felt too still, like something had pressed its weight onto the forest and nothing dared move under it.

Inside, Corwin sat by the hearth, holding the sketch again.

"I tried to burn it," he said. "But it wouldn't catch."

Elaine didn't take it from him. She just stared at the drawing. The door. The shadow. And now, something new. A mark in the corner. A spiral, like the one she'd seen carved into the Watcher's stone altar months ago.

The hunter came in with kindling. His face was darker than usual.

"We're not alone," he said.

Elaine looked up.

He set the wood down without meeting her eyes. "I tracked prints. Light ones. Around the back wall. They weren't there yesterday."

"Animal?" Corwin asked.

"No. Whatever it was stood. Watched. Didn't enter."

Elaine folded her arms. "Then why didn't it come in?"

The hunter finally met her gaze. "Because it doesn't need to. It's already inside."

They said nothing for a long time.

That evening, Corwin found a word carved into the table.

Not burned. Not inked. Carved.

REMAIN

Elaine ran her fingers over it. "Did you do this?"

Corwin shook his head slowly. "No."

The hunter leaned closer. "It's not a message. It's a command."

Elaine stared at the letters. Something about them felt wrong. Tilted. As if whoever had written it didn't understand how letters worked but had seen them enough to fake it.

Corwin whispered, "Maybe it wants us here."

Elaine turned to him sharply. "You said it. Not he."

Corwin blinked. "I don't know why."

That night, the dreams spread.

Elaine saw a house in the woods. The same house from Corwin's dream. No doors. No windows. But it breathed. Like something trapped inside wanted out.

She woke in a sweat. The hunter was already awake. Sitting. Watching the walls.

"You saw it too," she said.

He nodded once.

Elaine turned to the shadows in the corner of the room. They were darker than the rest of the cabin. Too dark.

Something had settled there.

And it wasn't planning to leave.

10

A Door Left Open

Elaine woke with the taste of iron in her mouth.

The fire had gone out. The air was wet with fog. Not mist — fog. The kind that swallowed sound and held onto breath.

Corwin was gone.

She was on her feet before her mind caught up. The hunter was already at the door.

"East," he said. "He went east. Into the woods."

Elaine grabbed her cloak and followed. The hunter said nothing more. They didn't run. They walked fast and silent (the kind of silence that belongs to hunters and mourners).

They found him near the edge of the treeline, standing before something half-sunken into the ground.

A structure.

Stone. Cracked. Covered in moss and ash. A wall with no sides. And in the center, the door from the sketches.

No frame. No hinges. Just a slab of black, leaning where no door should be.

Corwin didn't turn as they approached.

"I didn't mean to find it," he said. "I just kept walking. And it was here. Like it had been waiting."

Elaine stepped beside him. The air around the stone felt heavier.

"It's not real," the hunter said. But even he sounded unsure.

Corwin tilted his head. "It's listening."

Elaine looked at him. "Listening for what?"

"The lie we keep telling ourselves. That we're still safe."

The hunter moved closer. Touched the stone. Pulled back fast. Like it burned.

"It's a tether," he said. "One of its roots. It doesn't come here to hunt. It comes here to feed."

Elaine turned to him. "Can we break it?"

"Maybe. But it won't let us try without cost."

Corwin was still staring. His voice is softer now. "I think it wants to be opened."

Elaine grabbed his arm. "We're not opening anything. Not until we know what's inside."

Corwin didn't fight her. But he didn't step back either.

Elaine lingered at the door longer than the others. She stared at the stone until her breath felt tight in her chest.

She didn't trust it. Not the stone. Not the fog. Not the pull she saw in Corwin's eyes.

Back at the cabin, she paced.

The hunter watched her in silence. He had seen that look before. The one people wore just before they did something reckless. Or brave. Or both.

Elaine sat by the hearth, staring into the dead fire.

"I don't care what it wants," she said quietly. "I won't let it take him again."

The hunter poured water into the kettle. "That door's not just a thing, Elaine. It's a question. One you don't want answered."

She looked up. "Then we don't answer it. We board it. We bury it. We burn the forest around it if we have to."

He met her stare. "And what if it's not a door at all? What if it's a mirror?"

Elaine didn't reply. She wrapped her arms around herself, as if holding something in. Or holding something back.

Corwin didn't speak much that night. He just watched the fog thicken through the window. Every now and then, he blinked like waking from a dream he hadn't meant to enter.

Elaine didn't sleep. She sat in the corner of the room, knife in hand, watching the door.

If the Watcher wanted her brother back, it would have to get through her.

They returned to the cabin. The fog followed.

That night, the word on the table had changed.

REMAIN had become **RETURN**.

And outside, in the woods, something stood in the shape of Corwin.

But its eyes were too still.

11
What Follows the Shape

The thing in the woods didn't move.

Elaine watched it from the window, breath held. It stood where the fog met the trees. Still. Unblinking. And though it wore Corwin's outline, something in her gut curled. It was wrong.

She turned to look at her brother. He was by the fire, drowsy but awake, unaware that his shadow had grown a body outside.

The hunter was already at the door.

"Stay back," he said.

Elaine stepped beside him. "That's not him."

"I know."

They opened the door.

Cold poured in like water. The fog shifted, pulling itself inward, like breath drawn slow and deliberate. The thing didn't flinch. Didn't speak.

Then, it turned.

And vanished into the woods.

The hunter didn't follow. He closed the door.

"Not tonight."

Elaine sat beside Corwin. He blinked at her, then looked around.

"Did I go outside again?"

"No."

His eyes stayed on hers. Searching. "Are you sure?"

She nodded. "You've been here the whole time."

But inside, something frayed. A thread pulling loose.

Later, she woke to the sound of scratching.

A slow, steady drag along the cabin wall. Then silence. Then again.

She rose with the knife. The hunter wasn't in his bedroll. She stepped outside.

Fog. Deeper now. The trees looked farther away than they should.

She turned the corner.

The hunter stood there, staring at the back wall.

Something was carved into the wood.

WELCOME BACK

Elaine's voice was a whisper. "What does it mean?"

The hunter didn't look at her. "It means it's not after him anymore. Not directly."

She frowned. "Then who?"

He looked at her then. And she understood.

"It's trying to break me."

He nodded.

"It's succeeding."

Neither of them moved. The fog coiled around their boots. The words on the wall seemed to deepen.

Behind them, Corwin cried out in his sleep. Just once.

Elaine didn't go to him.

She just watched the tree line.

And waited to see if her own shadow would follow her back.

12

The One Who Remembered

The fog didn't lift that morning.

Elaine found the hunter kneeling in the clearing behind the cabin, tracing something into the dirt. Not a ward. Not a trap. Just a circle, over and over, like he was trying to draw time still.

"What is it doing to you?" she asked.

He didn't look up. "It remembers me."

Elaine's voice caught. "You said you'd never faced it before."

"I lied."

He stood slowly. His eyes were darker than before. Not tired. Hollowed.

"It wasn't always a Watcher," he said. "Once, it was a man. Like me. Like anyone."

Elaine didn't speak.

"He lost someone. Like we all do. But he couldn't let go. He gave up everything to hold on — time, memory, even his name."

"What happened?"

"He opened a door."

The hunter looked into the trees.

"It was years ago. A place deeper than forest. I tried to stop him. He called me brother."

Elaine stepped back. "You never told me."

"I thought he'd forgotten me."

The words on the cabin wall twisted in her mind. WELCOME BACK.

Elaine whispered, "So it wasn't for Corwin."

The hunter didn't answer.

Inside, Corwin had begun to hum.

Low. Repetitive. The same broken tune over and over.

Elaine didn't recognize it.

But the hunter did.

He closed his eyes.

"It was our mother's song."

Elaine looked at him, shaken. "Is he... inside Corwin now?"

The hunter shook his head. "Not yet. But the door's open. It remembers me. It wants to finish what we started."

Elaine stared into the fog. Her voice quiet, but certain.

"Then we close it."

The hunter didn't nod. He didn't speak.

But for the first time, he looked afraid.

13
What Remains

Elaine didn't sleep. Not fully.

She drifted in and out, her body still, but her mind running through every crack in the walls. Every whisper in the dark. Every look from Corwin that lingered just a little too long — as if he were seeing through her instead of at her.

She sat by the fire until morning, watching its final embers collapse into ash.

What do you do when the person you love is still alive, but not whole? What do you protect, the part that's left or the part you remember?

She thought of a memory. One buried so deep it only surfaced when she was bone-tired and hollow:

She was twelve. Corwin had scraped his leg climbing the bluff by the old mill. He hadn't cried, not until they got home and he saw the blood. She'd sat him down, cleaned the wound with the steadiness of someone pretending not to be afraid.

He had looked at her, wide-eyed, trusting.

"You always know what to do," he had whispered.

She didn't. Not then. Not now. But back then, it had been enough to pretend.

She blinked. The memory vanished.

Corwin stirred beside her. Still asleep, but his mouth moved, forming words she couldn't hear.

She leaned in. A whisper. A hum. That same tune.

The hunter came in with a pile of firewood. Set it down without a word.

Elaine looked up. "You said it remembers you."

"It does."

"Then why come back?"

He paused. Then: "Because if it's looking for me, it'll stop looking for him."

Elaine stood. "And what if it wants both now?"

He didn't answer.

The fog outside curled along the window like fingers.

Corwin sat up. Slowly. He looked at Elaine with eyes that were his, and not.

"I dreamed I walked into the dark," he said. "And the dark had my voice."

Elaine's jaw clenched. "You're not going back to that place."

He looked down at his hands. "What if I already did?"

She stepped closer. "Then we drag you back. Piece by piece, if we have to."

The hunter watched them, silent.

Elaine turned to him. "We shall close the door today. Before it opens on its own."

The hunter nodded.

But as they packed their things, Corwin stood still, watching the fog.

And the fog, somehow, watched back.

14
The Hollow Name

The walk to the door was slow.

Elaine kept her blade close. The hunter carried salt in his palm like a priest ready to banish ghosts. Corwin walked behind them, too quiet, the kind of quiet that wasn't rest — it was restraint.

They reached the stone slab. The door. It hadn't moved. But it hadn't aged either. Its edges were sharp as memory, its surface black like oil that never dried.

The hunter stepped forward.

"This is where it began."

Elaine turned to him. "What do you mean?"

He traced the air, and his hand drew a spiral — not a circle. Not a loop. A spiral that tightened inward.

"This is not just a door. It's a Sigil of Reversal. It wasn't built to open. It was built to reflect."

Elaine stared. "Reflect what?"

He looked at Corwin.

"Whatever you bring to it. Grief. Anger. Love. It shows it back — changed. Twisted. It doesn't give you power. It gives you proof that your pain matters. Enough to rot you from the inside out."

Elaine took a step back. "And the Watcher?"

The hunter's jaw clenched.

"He came here when he was still my brother. He had lost someone. A daughter. Maybe a son. He never said. Just that the world felt too cruel for someone so small."

He stared at the stone.

"He stood before this door and carved his name out of himself. That was the trade. Memory for power. Love for permanence."

Elaine whispered, "And you didn't stop him."

"I tried. But the door offered something I couldn't. It told him he could remember without hurting. That he could love without losing."

Corwin stepped closer.

"And what does it want now?"

The hunter looked at him. "It wants a vessel. A story. A mirror that bleeds."

Elaine pulled Corwin back.

"So we burn it. We break the reflection."

The hunter shook his head.

"You can't burn something that remembers what fire feels like. You can't break a door that opens inward."

He reached into his coat. Pulled out a small bone disc etched with symbols. Circles within spirals. A sigil burned into ivory.

"This is the mark of the Hollow. Those who gave up their names to keep a memory alive. There are more of them. Across the world. Quiet. Watching."

Elaine's voice was low. "So your brother wasn't the only one."

"No," the hunter said. "But he was the first to turn back. And now he wants to pull the rest of us through."

Corwin touched the stone. Just once.

And it pulsed.

Elaine shouted, pulled him away. He blinked, dazed, and for a second — just one — his eyes glowed with something ancient.

The hunter threw the bone disc at the door.

It shattered.

Not the door. The disc.

The door stayed still.

And somewhere in the trees, the fog laughed.

Elaine gripped her knife tighter.

"Then we find a way. Because I won't let him become someone I have to fight."

The hunter looked at her like someone who had once said the same.

Final Act

15

The Choice

Elaine woke to silence.

Corwin was gone.

She tore through the cabin. His bedroll was cold. The knife he kept near his side was missing. The door left open, fog curling like fingers across the threshold.

She didn't scream. She didn't call for him. She just ran.

The hunter met her halfway through the woods. He didn't ask where she was going. He already knew.

They reached the door in minutes. This time, it was different.

Open.

No sound. No light. Just the shape of absence. And Corwin, standing at its edge.

He turned when they arrived. Calm. Collected. Too calm.

"You came," he said.

Elaine stepped forward, careful. "You don't have to do this."

Corwin didn't move. "I remember now. The dreams. The river. Your face. But they're like stories I overheard. Not memories. Just echoes."

Elaine's throat clenched. "That's enough. It's still something."

"Not for me." His eyes softened. "Don't you see? This door... it doesn't just steal. It offers."

The hunter spoke, low and rough. "You don't know what it's offering."

Corwin looked at him. "I think I do. I've seen what it gave you. What it took. And you've been carrying it ever since."

Elaine stepped between them. "You're not going in."

Corwin smiled, not cruel, but tired. "I already have."

And he stepped backward.

Into the dark.

The door didn't close.

It simply absorbed him.

Elaine ran to it, but the hunter caught her.

"No," he said, voice breaking. "Not yet."

She collapsed to her knees.

Not screaming. Just silent.

The door pulsed once. Then stilled.

Elaine pressed her forehead to the stone.

"Then I'll bring him back."

She stood.

And for the first time, the hunter didn't stop her.

16

What the Fog Remembers

Elaine stepped through.

No sound. No light. Not even cold. Just the sense of un-being, like falling through yourself.

And then the world snapped back.

She stood in a forest that wasn't theirs. The trees lean inward. Their bark shimmered, not with life, but with memory. Faces. Moments. A boy chasing fireflies. A girl crying into her cloak. All burned into wood.

She turned. The door was gone.

So was the hunter.

So was her name.

It took a moment to remember it. Elaine. She said it out loud just to keep it from slipping.

Something moved through the trees.

Not Corwin. Something wearing his voice.

"You shouldn't be here."

She ran toward the sound, and the forest twisted. Branches rearranged. Paths changed shape.

Elaine stumbled into a clearing. A figure stood there, back turned.

Corwin.

No. Not quite.

He turned.

His eyes weren't his. They were mirrors. And in them, she saw herself, older. Hardened. Eyes like flint.

"What are you?" she whispered.

The figure stepped forward. Voice still his. "I am the memory of who you failed to save."

Elaine raised her knife. It didn't gleam. Light had no meaning here.

"Where's the real Corwin?"

"He's walking," the echo said. "Through every memory he ever buried. And when he stops... there won't be anything left of him that remembers you."

Elaine clenched her jaw.

"Then I'll walk faster."

The forest shuddered.

And behind her, a shadow peeled off a tree.

It was the Watcher.

But this time, he didn't lunge.

He bowed.

"You came back," he said.

Elaine didn't flinch. "You took him."

"I offered. He chose."

"What do you want from me?"

He straightened. "Not want. Need."

His voice was cracked glass, but his face was calm. "He was never the story. You are."

Elaine said nothing.

But her hand found the hilt of her blade. Not to defend.

To remember the weight of it.

The Watcher smiled. "Now we begin."

17
The Quiet Becoming

Elaine walked for hours without marking the path. The trees didn't stay still. The air pulsed like breath. But she didn't ask questions anymore.

She had stopped needing the world to make sense.

There was a stream that spoke in riddles. A sky that flickered between dusk and dawn. And still, no sign of Corwin.

She drank from nothing. Ate nothing. Slept when the memories let her.

At first, she dreamed of him. His laugh. His scars. The shape of his hand reaching back toward hers. Then the dreams changed. He wasn't in them. Only her. Walking. Holding a knife. A face hard as bone.

She stopped crying the third day.

Not because she didn't hurt. But because the tears didn't change the fog.

The Watcher followed at a distance.

He never attacked. Never spoke.

Only watched.

One night, he appeared beside her. No sound. No malice.

"I remember when you were small," he said. "You used to sing to the river."

Elaine stared ahead. "You remember wrong."

"I remember better."

She turned to him. "Why me?"

"Because you are a story that refuses to end."

She walked faster.

On the seventh day, the forest opened without warning.

No trail. No sound. Just absence — like the woods themselves exhaled and left a hollow behind.

In the clearing, a tree stood alone.

Not ancient. Not glowing. Just... present. Its bark was the color of ash, and its branches curled back toward the trunk like arms shielding a wound.

Elaine approached it slowly. Something about it felt wrong. Not dangerous — just familiar in a way she couldn't place.

She touched the bark. It didn't burn. But her memories twisted.

Not visions. Distortions.

She saw Corwin as a child — laughing, bleeding, fading.

She saw herself — older, colder, with eyes that didn't flinch.

Inside the bark were faces. Not glowing. Just carved, like someone had spent decades trying to remember by force.

Her own was there. And yet... not. Eyes were wrong. Mouth was too still.

She stepped back.

From the leaves above, a voice whispered:

"You are not here to save him. You are here to become him."

Elaine's hands shook. Her blade didn't.

She carved her name into the trunk anyway.

Not to make a mark.

To remember what her hands felt like.

Behind her, the Watcher laughed softly. "You're beginning to understand."

Elaine whispered, "If I lose everything to save him... and he forgets me again, what am I?"

The Watcher touched the bark beside her name. "Then you are the root of him. The cost. The myth. The martyr."

She didn't scream.

She just walked on.

And the fog followed.

18
The Hollowing

Elaine forgot what her voice sounded like.

She hadn't spoken in days. Or maybe it had only been hours. Time didn't stretch here — it spiraled, curling in on itself like the sigil carved into the door.

She walked. That was the only constant.

Each step felt heavier. Not from exhaustion, but from memory. The forest remembered every place her foot had landed before. It whispered back the weight.

She came across a shallow pond, still as stone. Her reflection blinked.

But she hadn't.

Elaine leaned closer.

The face staring back wasn't hers. Not fully. The eyes were flint. The mouth unreadable. But what shattered her breath was the knife — not in her hand, but her reflection's mouth. Gripped like a secret.

She stepped back. The water rippled once. Then stilled.

The Watcher sat by a dead tree nearby. Not watching her. Watching the reflection.

"You're almost ready," he said.

Elaine's voice cracked like frost. "For what?"

"To give something you won't get back. The final thread. The name inside your name."

She sat across from him. "What does that mean?"

He gestured to the water. "Say your name. Then watch."

She hesitated. Then whispered, "Elaine."

The reflection smiled. But her lips hadn't moved.

The Watcher stood. "You still think this is about him. It's not. It never was. It's about the version of you that dies here... so another can carry the weight."

Elaine stared into the water again.

The reflection was gone.

Just fog now.

And then — a sound.

A voice. Corwin's. Distant. Raw.

"ELAINE....don't."

She turned.

The forest opened.

She ran toward it.

Branches clawed her skin. Stones bit her heels. But she didn't stop.

She burst into a clearing.

Corwin stood there.

Older. Weathered. And for the first time.... afraid.

He stepped back. "You shouldn't be here."

"I came for you."

"You don't know what that means anymore."

She took a breath. "Then show me."

And she stepped closer.

This time, the Watcher didn't follow.

This time, he watched something else begin to fade.

19

The Name That Burns

The clearing was too quiet.

Not still , empty. Like something had taken sound and wrung it dry.

Corwin stood with his hands at his sides, eyes haunted. The lines on his face weren't age. They were choices.

Elaine stepped forward, and he stepped back.

"I don't remember the river anymore," he said. "Or the sound your boots made on wood. I know your face, but not what it means."

Elaine's voice was low. "Then let me remind you."

Corwin shook his head. "You don't get it. I chose to forget. The door didn't steal it. I gave it away."

She froze.

"I remembered what it felt like when you cried in the dark, and I couldn't help. I remembered the way you held me when I shook like a dying thing. I remembered the day you bled for me and smiled like it didn't matter."

He swallowed hard.

"And I realized... I couldn't carry that anymore."

Elaine's legs trembled. "So you let go of me?"

"I let go of being a wound."

A wind passed through the clearing. The trees bowed slightly.

Elaine stepped forward. "I crossed the door for you. I let go of my name. My voice. Everything. You're all I had left."

He closed his eyes. "Then you should've stopped before you broke."

She fell to her knees.

The weight caught up to her , not just grief, but the grief she chose.

"I didn't come to save you," she said. "I came to give you back the part of me I didn't know how to live without."

Corwin didn't move.

"I carved my name into the tree because I was forgetting it. I let the Watcher follow me because I thought if I could suffer enough... maybe I deserve your memory."

Her voice cracked. "And I thought if you saw me now, you'd know I never stopped loving you."

Corwin knelt beside her. But not close. Not close enough.

He looked at her hands, bloodied, dirt-caked, trembling.

"Maybe I do know that," he said.

Elaine looked up, hope flickering.

"But it doesn't bring back the person I was. And it won't bring back the person you were either."

She broke.

Not loud. Not screaming.

She broke like glass in a gloved hand, quietly, finally.

The forest didn't echo.

The Watcher watched.

And for the first time, he turned away.

Elaine whispered into the ground, not for him, not for the Watcher, not even for the world.

Just for herself.

"I don't want to be remembered. I want to rest.

20

The Thread That Remains

Days passed. Maybe weeks. The forest no longer marked them.

Elaine and Corwin didn't speak often. Not out of anger. There was simply nothing left to say that hadn't already hollowed them.

The fog receded. The door, the true door, stood where it always had, unchanging.

Elaine stood before it one last time. No longer to go through. But to let go.

The Watcher waited. He always did.

"You kept your thread," he said.

She looked at him, exhausted. "What are you really?"

The Watcher tilted his head. "A witness. A memory that chose not to fade. Your brother made me. So did you."

Corwin stepped forward. "Then end it."

The Watcher looked at him, amused. "You misunderstand. I don't trap people. I give them somewhere to put their pain. You came willingly. So did she."

Elaine stepped closer. "Then take mine."

The Watcher paused. "And leave you with what?"

She closed her eyes. "Nothing. That's the point."

But Corwin took her hand.

"No," he said. "She keeps it. We both do. Because forgetting didn't heal me. And remembering didn't save her."

Elaine opened her eyes. Looked at him.

The Watcher smiled. "Then walk. Go on. Try again."

They turned from the door.

The forest let them leave.

When they reached the edge, the hunter stood waiting. Older. Thin. Scarred by something they couldn't see.

He didn't speak. Just nodded once.

Elaine nodded back.

The three walked on.

Behind them, the door closed.

And somewhere deep beneath it, something cracked.

Not broken.

Just... waiting.

For the next story.

The Map

The Known Land ends at the Forest of Threads, a place not mapped in ink but in forgetting. Beyond its fog is the Watcher's Door, the threshold between memory and myth. There's also the Hollow Peaks that towers over the treeline and the river that is called Duskfall.

Rest, you can decipher if you have read this book completely!

Enter Caption

Before the Watcher was memory, he was a man. A father. A brother. A name now lost to time and pain.

It is said he came to the Sigil Door not to seek power, but to erase something too heavy to carry, the death of a child, or perhaps the slow unmaking of someone he loved. Grief cracked his spirit open, and the Door, ever listening, offered silence in return.

But silence never comes free.

To forget, he surrendered his name. To unfeel, he gave up the shape of his face. What remained was a being built from echoes, a presence that feeds not on flesh, but on remembrance. The Watcher does not hunt. He waits. And waits. And waits. Because grief always circles back.

Those who encounter him speak of eyes that reflect their worst memories. Of voices spoken in familiar tones. Of calmness that feels like drowning.

Some say the Watcher envies the Hollowed, those who chose forgetting completely. Others believe he guards the Door to ensure no one follows him through. But the truth is simpler:

The Watcher is not evil. He is not kind. He is the cost of remembering too much.

Key Locations

- **The Sigil Door:**
A black stone gate that opens inward, not outward. Those who enter do not leave unchanged.
- **The Forest of Threads:**
A living place that remembers every footfall. Time does not pass here. It repeats.
- **The Memory Tree:**
Found only by those unraveling. Its bark records echoes, not facts.
- **The Clearing of Mirrors:**
Where truth wears familiar faces.
- **The Bleeding Path:**
A narrow trail through the forest that appears only during personal surrender. It is said to reflect one's deepest sacrifice.
- **Duskfall:**
A stream said to remove all memory from those who drink from it. Some search for it. Others run from it.
- **The Stone of Names:**
A weathered boulder marked by generations of Hollowed. Each name carved into it was once a person who chose to forget.
- **The Still House:**
A ruin hidden deep within the forest, where time halts. The Watcher is believed to return here when silence grows too loud. A black stone gate that opens inward, not outward. Those who enter do not leave unchanged.

Glossary Of Echoes

- **The Watcher**: Once human. Now memory itself. Feeds on grief but offers clarity.
- **The Hollowed**: Those who gave up names to hold onto a moment. Neither alive nor lost.
- **The Thread**: The last part of someone that holds meaning, identity, sacrifice, or love.
- **Elaine**: The girl who crossed for love. Who stayed until her name thinned into story.
- **Corwin**: Her brother. The wound. The mirror. The memory that let go.
- **The Hunter**: Once brother to the Watcher. Now the shadow that survives aftermath.

Connect With The Author

Thank you for reading **The Thread That Remains**.

If this story stayed with you, I'd love to hear from you.

You can reach out or follow upcoming projects at:

? ghatakanish1@gmail.com

? Instagram: @knightin_black

Every review, message, or shared line means more than you know. The thread continues, in words, in memory, in connection.

Coming Soon

The Thread That Breaks

A return to the door.

A memory that shouldn't have survived.

A name that was never truly forgotten.

Stay tuned.